An Angel in my Shadow

By Jerry Raaf

Mill Lake Books

Mill Lake Books
Chilliwack, BC, Canada
https://jamescoggins.wordpress.com/mill-lake-books/

Cover design by Dean Tjepkema

ISBN: 978-1-7771926-4-8

A GIFT TO

____

FROM

____

DATE

____

This book honours the lives and memory
of

~ *Sanford & Isobel Hanson* ~

They provided me with
encouragement, love, and genuine
friendship
and trusted me with one of their own.
I miss them greatly.

Table of Contents

————————

Prologue

When the Right Reverend Doctor Donald G. McPhee bestowed the title of Canon upon Reverend Owen R. Richards during a synod meeting in Toronto, Canada, all the delegates stood to their feet and applauded as a sign of respect, support, and affirmation.

Shortly after, Owen's seven-year-old son, Geo, asked him what "Canon" meant, Owen smiled and whispered as he ruffled Geo's hair, "I guess it means that I am now a big shot."

It would be impossible to calculate the number of hours Owen had spent in seminary and Bible school libraries studying Hebrew, Greek, hermeneutics, apologetics, biblical history, and philosophy and reading theological works written by the likes of Martin Luther, Thomas Cranmer, and the historian Josephus. The Hebrew Tanakh, English/Greek interlinear texts, and biblical translations were among Owen's favourite books.

Owen had also enjoyed the practical side of his educational experience when he had served internships as a chaplain to Canadian military personnel and to inmates at two federal prisons. He had volunteered whatever time he could to community youth clubs and frequently visited nursing homes and local hospitals. On rare occasions, a local police department had called on him to assist with troubled citizens.

During the past twelve years, he had served as an assistant priest in four Anglican congregations in Great Britain, the United States, and Canada. Eventually, Owen had been called to an Anglican church where his friendly demeanour, his relationship skills, and his ease in public settings had ultimately earned him promotion to Senior Rector.

When asked what were the most significant lessons he had learned over his years of study, he would smile as he opened his left hand. With the pointer finger on his right hand, he would touch one finger at a time and say, "Number one, keep in touch with God at all times. Number two, be patient with others and yourself. Number three, learn to accept change. Above all else, do not be intimidated by the unusual because there are many things that you will experience that they never taught you in seminary."

His extensive experience in prison ministries and substance abuse rehab centres had exposed him to the deterioration of cultural and societal life, which in time had begun to tax his inner fibre. Phone calls from the police department to attend distasteful murder scenes and tragic suicides had prompted him to question his mandate to help people. Often, he would think about relocating to an isolated town farther removed from the worst forms of human depravity. There was even a time when he had considered applying for a position as a lighthouse keeper on an isolated corner of Canada's coastline.

Whenever his cup was full of stressful events and seemingly hopeless situations, he would drive to the riverbank and listen to the birds that warbled and chirped in such a peaceful place. After a prayer, he would sit in the park next to several large oak trees and listen to the leaves rustling in the warm breeze.

Often, he would tell God how he felt about all the violence and evil around him, and in one of his prayers he had asked God for a sign that he could be relieved from his duties to humanity. He would pray, "This place is a spiritual junkyard, and now I know what it was like to have lived in Noah's day. People are angry, greedy, violent, and arrogant, haters of each other and God. I know You made man and his descendants, but my question is the one stated in Psalm 8:4: 'What is mankind that you are mindful of them, human beings that you care for them?' You have demonstrated that You are patient, slow to anger, and plenteous in mercy."

____

Chapter 1
An Unexpected Guest

The antique grandfather clock on the main floor of the home of the Reverend Owen Richards began to peal the Westminster chimes. It began with the usual sixteen notes, paused, and then counted the hours in a deep, reverberating, mellow tone: BONG BONG BONG. This sustained, rich, echoing sound bravely challenged the darkness possessing the main floor hallway before fading into the surrounding silence. Freckles, the family Dalmatian, raised his head and yawned before returning to his former position of comfort on the lush carpet next to the brick fireplace.

When silence had returned to the home, Owen stirred and opened his tired eyes as he pulled the covers to his chin. After several prolonged breaths, he became aware that the wind chimes, hanging on the patio just below his bedroom window, were ringing as though there was an intense wind outside. Owen pushed the covers aside, sat up, and adjusted his eyes to the surrounding darkness. Moments later, he began his nocturnal journey to the washroom. Returning to the bedroom, he could still hear the wind chimes loudly ringing, so he parted the drapes slightly to see how blustery it was outside. Surprised, he peered into the shadowy backyard to see that all of the bushes and the limbs of the trees were still, yet the chimes were continuing to peal their ghostly summons. Owen's eyes searched the darkened backyard for the cause of the continuous ringing. Nothing seemed unusual, and yet there seemed to be a shadowy something or someone seated on the decorative garden bench next to the pathway leading to the coy pond.

Owen rubbed his eyes before studying the figure of what appeared to be an elderly man in his backyard. The legs of this alien creature, seated on the ornate bench, were stretched out and crossed at the ankles, and his arms were extended in opposite directions across the back of the bench. The stranger's head was tilted back as though he were looking up at the stars. He appeared to be resting and enjoying his comfortable position.

Wrinkling his brow, Owen resisted the urge to tap on the window. For several minutes, he stared intently at the uninvited guest to see if he recognized him. The stranger appeared friendly and did not show signs of being confrontational or troublesome, and he certainly did not give the impression that he was a homeless person. Try as he might, Owen did not recognize him as anyone from his congregation or his immediate neighbourhood.

Unsure of what to do, Owen reached behind him for one of the stuffed decorative chairs so that he could sit and watch the man. Sitting down, he scrutinized the well-dressed alien. He certainly did not look like a vagrant because his clothes did not appear to be tattered, and his white hair and beard were neatly trimmed. It was difficult to speculate how tall he was because of the darkness and the seated position he was in.

The antique clock chimed again, indicating that fifteen minutes had passed.

To Owen's surprise, the garden guest stood to his feet, stretched, and yawned before waving at Owen—as if he knew he was being watched. Then he walked toward the locked gate in the fence that led to the alley.

Owen seemed mesmerized and unable to move. He was unaware of how long he had been seated by the window when something nudged his knee. From habit, he instinctively reached down to scratch the ears of Freckles, the friendly family pet. Startled by his wife's voice, Owen stood to his feet and returned to sit on the edge of the bed.

"Are you okay, dear?" Helen whispered as she reached for his pillow to fluff it up. "You act like you've seen a ghost. Were you having a bad dream?"

"It's hard to...to explain what I've seen." His voice momentarily quivered as he tried to convince himself that seeing the stranger had not been a dream. "How did he walk through the locked gate without opening it with a key?" Owen mumbled to himself.

Helen knelt on the mattress behind him and massaged his neck. "Lie down, dear, and try to get some sleep," she whispered as she began to yawn.

"The wind chimes—did you hear them ringing?" asked Owen.

"Now that you mention it, yes. But they're silent now. Did they wake you?"

"I don't recall," Owen responded as he laid his head on the pillow.

"What were you looking at?" Helen asked as she reclined next to him.

"There is...I mean, there was a white-haired man in our backyard, and he was sitting on the garden bench next to the coy pond."

"A white-haired man in our backyard? Should we call the police?" She breathed nervously as her eyes darted toward the drapes.

"No. He looked rather harmless and left the yard through the back gate."

"But it is locked, isn't it?" A moment passed before she whispered, "Well, who is he?"

"I don't know. I've never seen him before, on the street or in any of the stores and shops, certainly not in our congregation. I don't know who he is." Owen sighed loudly as he ran his fingers through his hair.

"Are you sure?" she asked. "Why did he choose our yard?"

"If I knew that, I would know his name and where he comes from." There was no hint of confrontation in his response.

Just then, the grandfather clock boldly chimed again: BONG BONG BONG BONG.

Owen closed his eyes and took in an extended breath before yawning, but sleep did not come to him. The image of the well-dressed alien seemed to mock him. It had left an indelible imprint in his mind.

"How did he walk through the back gate without a key to the lock? I'm sure I locked it yesterday," whispered Owen.

———

Chapter 2
An Unsettling Day

Owen stared at the dark ceiling until morning light began to creep through the small spaces around the bedroom drapes. When he heard the grandfather clock indicate seven o'clock, Owen tossed back the covers and sat up. He shaved, washed his face, and reached for his bottle of aftershave. Then he donned his black trousers and his shirt with the white clerical collar and went downstairs to the kitchen. He poured himself a coffee and sat at the island in the centre of the kitchen.

"Your breakfast is almost ready, dear," Helen said as she turned to pour a glass of milk for Geo, their eight-year-old son.

"Good morning, son. Did you sleep well?" Owen asked as he brushed Geo's hair with his hand.

"I heard the wind chimes this morning. Was there a wind?" asked Geo as he reached for the milk.

Owen poked at the poached egg on toast that Helen had prepared for him, but he was preoccupied with what he had seen in the backyard.

"Are you alright?" Helen asked again as she pulled up a chair to sit next to him. She stirred her coffee and waited for his response

"I haven't seen that man before," Owen said in a hushed tone.

"What man?"

"The one I saw in our backyard," Owen responded. Moments later, he turned to look at Helen. "I've thought about that man, and I'm sure I've never seen him before."

"May I leave the table, Mom?" Geo asked.

Helen nodded her approval, and as Geo carried his plate to the sink, she said, "Thank you, Geo."

Geo left the kitchen, and Helen continued to stir her coffee. She had apparently decided not to engage with Owen over what he had seen in the backyard. She watched the steam rise from her mug, pursed her lips, and allowed her breath to blow across the surface to cool it.

They sat in silence for several moments before Owen spoke. "Thank you for breakfast." He kissed her forehead, got up, opened the back door, and stepped out onto the patio. Walking slowly and cautiously toward the garden bench, he searched the area for clues that would indicate that someone had been there. After several moments, he turned and walked toward the gate in the backyard fence. When he arrived next to the gate, he tugged gently on it and found it firmly closed and locked.

Returning to the house and entering his office adjacent to the kitchen, Owen slumped into his padded chair and reached for the Bible on his desk. Thumbing through the New Testament, he started to read Hebrews 13, beginning with verse 1: "Keep on loving one another as brothers and sisters." But it was verse 2 that caught his attention: "Do not forget to show hospitality to strangers, for by so doing some people have shown hospitality to angels without knowing it." Owen read the verse several times and raised his eyes to stare blankly at the family portrait on the wall. The pages of the Bible slid silently shut as he thought about the alien in the backyard. "Could it be?" he asked himself.

His prayer was simple and earnest. "Almighty God, I believe Your Word and wait for Your instructions to me for this day. What do You wish me to learn from this verse and from last night's experience? You have told us not to be afraid, so today I place myself in Your hands. Amen."

He sat in silence. Some time later, he heard the grandfather clock strike eight o'clock, so he stood to his feet, walked into the kitchen, and kissed Helen's cheek. Before entering the garage, he thanked Helen again for breakfast and hugged Geo, who was donning his favourite jacket. Freckles nudged him, so he reached down to scratch his ears. Owen offered to drive Geo to school, but a friend of his had just arrived with his BMX bicycle, so both lads mounted their bicycles and pedaled away.

Before closing the door to the garage, Owen shouted to Helen, "Dear, before I go to the church, I plan to stop for a haircut at Lou's. I'll call you later."

Owen backed the car out of the garage and started for the barbershop. At the intersection of Morgan and Hillsborough, he moved into the righthand lane to make his turn. While waiting for a green light, he turned his head to the left to see how much traffic was approaching. At that moment, something at the bus stop caught his eye. In the middle of the crowd waiting for a bus stood a white-haired man, identical to the man who had been in his backyard.

Owen waited for the traffic light to turn green, but a horn sounded behind him, so he quickly looked both ways before rounding the corner. He turned right again and drove around the block to return to the bus stop, but three buses were leaving by the time he arrived, so he was unable to see which bus the white-haired man had boarded.

Owen glanced at his wristwatch before driving on to Lou's Barbershop. After finding a parking spot, he put the vehicle into park, turned off the engine, unlatched his seatbelt, and exited the car. His eyes immediately fell onto two men standing near the entrance of the barbershop. Both men, were holding up religious magazines. The older man smiled and approached Owen.

"Good morning, sir. You appear to be a man of the cloth."

Owen smiled as he nodded in the affirmative.

"May I have a few moments of your time?" asked the older gentleman.

Placing his keys in his pocket, Owen glanced at the magazines the man held in his hand. "Yes, it is a day that the Lord has made. What can I do for you?"

"I perceive from your clerical collar that you are a religious man."

Owen smiled, and looked into the man's face. "I don't consider myself to be religious. However, I am a believer in Jesus Christ. Are you a believer?"

"Do you believe in the Trinity?" asked the man as he lowered the hand holding *Watchtower* magazines.

"As a matter of fact, I do," responded Owen.

"You are aware that the word 'Trinity' does not exist in the scriptures? There is no such word in the Bible. It seems to have been invented later."

"You are correct, but there are verses in the original texts that suggest that there are three entities to God, the Father, the Son, and the Holy Spirit, who exist together in unity yet are one God."

"Where are these verses?"

"I am not familiar with your religious texts because they have been known to have been altered several times, but Matthew 28 commands believers to spread the good news to all people, teaching them and baptizing them in the name of the Father and of the Son and of the Holy Spirit. These three are clearly listed and identified."

"Not everyone believes that," the man responded.

"I understand, but false teachings exist in many denominations. One large group has in its tenets that Jesus and Satan are brothers and that is why there is conflict between good and evil."

The man leaned against Owen's vehicle and cast his gaze toward the sky. "Maybe there are four in this essence of God."

"Four? What gave you that idea?"

"At the end of the block is a large church that influences millions around the world. Its followers pray to a woman they call the Mother of God. So, does that mean that there is God the Father, Mary the Mother of God, the Son, and the Holy Spirit? That makes a family of four." He crossed his arms, and his body moved into a confrontational stance.

"If you're trying to have me speak against any church, its beliefs or doctrine, I'm sorry but I will not have you put words into my mouth."

The younger man appeared to be uncomfortable and restless.

Owen continued, "Just because one person, who declared himself to be a leader, said something, it does not mean it is true. I mean you no harm or insult, but the ancient manuscripts are clear. If you would allow me to page through your version of the scriptures..."

"Do you believe that Mary is a god? Do you pray to her?" interrupted the man.

"No, but I respect her and her willingness to bear Jesus and to care for Him while he was a child."

"Are all of those people wrong for praying to her?"

"You are asking me to make a judgement on people and their religious practices. As a believer and follower of Jesus Christ, my task is not to judge people, their beliefs, or their practices."

"How much works must a person do to earn eternal life, if there is such a thing?"

"There is nothing you can do to earn eternal life or make God love you more, or less. Eternal life is a gift from God. The Bible tells us that if we try to earn eternal life, we will find that our efforts will fail. The scriptures are clear that our efforts and works are as filthy rags. If we confess Jesus Christ and believe in our heart that God raised him from the dead, we will be saved."

There was a long pause before the man responded. "Saved from what?"

"God's judgement. He has provided a way of escape, and all you have to do is believe, and if you believe in Jesus Christ, your life will be different."

Looking at his watch, the older man said, "Come, Brother Randy. We need to speak with Elder Watson."

Moments later, both the older man and the younger man walked away, leaving Owen to gaze into the barbershop window. All seats appeared to be occupied with waiting customers, so Owen re-entered his car and started for the church. Exiting his car in the church parking lot, he walked up to the door of the church as though he were in a trance.

"What was all that about? And who was that white-haired man in my backyard? Why does all of this vex me?" Owen kept repeating to himself.

Once inside the building, he entered his office. Amy, the church secretary, carried a cup of black coffee into Owen's office and placed it on the corner of his desk.

"I know it isn't my place to say anything, but you look like you've had a restless night. Are you alright?" she asked as she smiled and tilted her head to one side. She had a way of encouraging him with her smile.

"No, not really, but thanks for the coffee," he whispered as he reached for the cup. "Oh, by the way, good morning," he said, returning a smile.

She grinned and brushed her hair from her face. After Amy left his office, Owen searched for his appointment book and turned to the page that displayed his appointments for the day. Amy appeared at the door again and knocked gently. When he nodded his approval, she entered and sat in the stuffed chair across from him.

"Eleanor Gibbons and Angela Ringwald are in the hospital again," she said. "All arrangements have been completed for the church bake sale this Saturday, and, as you know, Reverend Edward is planning to be back from vacation, so he's willing to conduct the Sunday morning service."

"Anything else?" Owen asked as he raised his cup to his lips and gently blew across the surface to cool the coffee.

"Yes, I almost forgot. Dr. Steve Kramer, your physician, wants to have coffee with you this morning at Tim Horton's at about eleven o'clock. I have his cell number if you're unable to be there."

Just then, the telephone rang in Amy's office, so she excused herself and left the room. Owen walked to the window to look at the swaying branches of the trees and bushes outside. He stood in silence, recalling his experience earlier that morning.

"I wonder who that white-haired fellow is. I am certain that I don't know him. He has never been in the congregation that I know of. And why was he waving at me? Why did he choose to leave my backyard through the locked gate into the alley? And how did he do it?" Several minutes passed as Owen relived what he had seen at three a.m. that morning.

Amy returned to his office, "Is there anything you need?"

"Yes, Amy. Please telephone Eleanor and Angela's families to see how urgent my visit is at the hospital."

She closed the door, leaving him to his private prayers.

He looked at the tiny clock on his desk and saw that it was 10:30. Then he closed his eyes and began his morning prayer. "Abba, Father, assist me this day to be kind and gracious to all I meet and speak with. May the words of my mouth be healing and encouraging even as Your Son Jesus Christ my Lord's words were kind, and may my actions assist others who are in need. I request Your wisdom and sensitivity because I do not know what I will encounter or who I will be speaking with this day. And whoever that white-haired man is, help me to be patient, gracious, and understanding—if we meet. Amen."

When he had finished his prayer, Owen reached for his cell phone, a New Testament Bible, and a small notepad before starting for the parking lot. He did not speak with Amy because she was in the photocopy room, so he just closed the door of the church and reached into his pocket for his car keys as he crossed the parking lot.

When he arrived at Tim Horton's for his appointment with Dr. Kramer, Owen had to search for a parking spot because there were more than twenty black Harley-Davidson motorcycles parked adjacent to the entrance. He stopped to admire several of the motorcycles as he walked among them. When he stepped inside the coffee shop, he saw that the line-up stretched all the way to the door. He scanned the seating area to see if Steve was there but did not see him. Just then, his cell phone rang. Turning suddenly to answer it, he bumped into one of the bikers, knocking the coffee from his hand.

"Oh, I'm so sorry," Owen said as he looked up into the face of a bearded biker.

The large, leather-clad young man suddenly grabbed Owen's shirt just below his chin.

"I'm sorry. I'll buy you another coffee. I never meant to..."

"Listen, padre," growled the biker, his eyes glaring with anger as he pulled one hand back and clenched it into a fist.

An older and shorter biker, who was standing nearby, turned and snarled at the bearded young man. "Leave the padre alone," he growled. "He said he'd buy you another coffee, so give him some respect."

"But he..."

"I said leave the padre alone!" His voice was strong and commanding.

Owen stepped to the counter and purchased a large black coffee, which he handed to the angry biker.

After stepping outside, Owen took an extended breath before walking to his car. He unlocked the door, climbed inside, and reached for the seatbelt. Before starting the engine, he looked over at the coffee shop entrance, and there stood the white-haired man, who waved at him. Owen blinked his eyes, somewhat dazed. A couple of cars turned into the parking lot, coming between Owen and the man, and blocked his view. When they had passed, Owen looked again, and the white-haired man was gone. After sitting there silently for several minutes, Owen started the car, left the parking lot, and drove directly to the church.

"So much for a quiet cup of coffee," he mumbled to himself as he turned down Calico Street.

When he arrived in the church foyer, Amy smiled at him. "Dr. Kramer just called and apologized for not being able to meet you for coffee. Apparently, he had an emergency at the hospital. I tried your cell phone, but I guess you didn't hear it."

"Oh. I heard it, but…"

Owen closed the door of his office and sat with his eyes closed. "What's going on?" he asked himself as he leaned back and breathed deeply.

There was a gentle rap on his door, so he responded. "Please come in."

Amy's face appeared at the partially open door. "Are you okay, sir?" she asked as she smiled.

"What is it?"

"I called the Gibbons and the Ringwald families. A visit would be appreciated later this evening or tomorrow if you're not too busy."

Owen nodded in the affirmative as she closed the door to his office. As he closed his eyes, he recalled his three encounters with the white-haired man. He folded his hands and nervously whispered, "Lord, now what?" Owen sat in silence for some time. "Who is this man, and why has he crossed my path three times within the last few hours? Is he a messenger from You? If he is, what message am I to hear? If all of this is not important, please ease my mind. If it is something critical, teach me what to do or say when I meet him. Amen." His voice faded into silence.

After reading his e-mails and studying an extensive memo from the area bishop, Owen went into the kitchen to refill his cup with black coffee. Returning to his office, he reread the weekly memos which Amy had prepared for all members and adherents of the church.

At 3:30 p.m., Owen walked down the hallway to the sanctuary. Seeing no one in the pews, he walked to the altar and knelt at the rail for prayer. During his silent contemplation, he had the distinct feeling that someone was watching him, so he slowly turned his head to look at the empty pews. There in a rear pew sat the white-haired man he had seen in his backyard, at the bus stop, and at the coffee shop.

———————————

Chapter 3
The Rendezvous

Owen's heartbeat quickened as he slowly stood to his feet, turned, and nodded courteously to the white-haired guest seated in the pew at the back of the sanctuary. The man smiled and returned a nod of acknowledgement. It seemed to Owen that the man's eyes had the ability to see through him, and yet his smile was friendly, and he appeared to be approachable. The closer Owen came to the man, the more difficult he found it to look into his eyes.

"I'm…I'm Owen," he stammered. "Who are you?"

The gentleman respectfully extended his right hand. "Yes, I know who you are, Owen. I've known you for thirty-seven years."

"You have?" Owen responded. "Thirty-seven years?" Owen narrowed his eyes to study the features of the man's face. At that moment,

Owen's hands felt cold, and he sensed perspiration on his brow.

After several moments of deafening silence, the man smiled. "Yes, I have known you for as long as you have been alive."

There was an uncomfortable pause as Owen momentarily glanced down at the floor. He tried to smile, but his face seemed stiff and unable to move. "But who are you?" asked Owen, surprised to hear his voice quiver.

"I am a servant of Adonai, the Lord Most High. Humans refer to Him as God."

During the silence that followed, Owen tried to breathe.

The white-haired man continued. "I have been assigned to be your guardian from the day of your conception."

"Really? You're my guardian angel?"

"Yes, I rode with your mother to a distant hospital on a motorized railway cart on an extremely cold day when the roads were impassible because of deep snow."

"What am I to say?" Owen whispered as he stepped back. His mind was racing, and he felt as if his chest would burst. "What is your name?"

"I respond to El Bashan," the man said as his smile momentarily eased Owen's fear. "I mean you no harm, Owen." His voice was strong and reassuring.

"You've known me all that time?" Owen's hand smoothed back his hair as his eyes focused on a blank spot on the wall behind the white-haired man.

"Yes, I have been assigned to be your protector so no harm would come to you. Many events have occurred throughout the years which have kept me busy tending to you."

Silence held Owen's tongue as he continued to stare at the blank spot on the wall.

El Bashan continued. "There were many times when you were in danger and never knew about it. Who do you think protected you today at the coffee shop?"

Several moments later, Owen managed to ask, "Tell me. Where are you from, and how long have you been here?"

"Owen, time means little to me. I don't know when I was created, nor do I have timelines to meet, but I have been assigned to protect you, and I have been mandated to be your guardian all these years."

"You have?" Owen slumped down into an adjacent pew. "If you have been near me all these years, why have I not seen you before?" Owen breathed deeply before continuing. "Why have I not had an opportunity to speak with you before?"

"You may not have seen me, but that does not mean I have not watched over you. When you were a youth, you did not receive serious injuries from that motorcycle accident, and when you were violently ill with appendicitis and other illnesses, it was I who watched over you."

Owen sat in silence as he recalled those unpleasant memories.

"Adonai chose you before your birth, and when you were an adolescent, He made known His desire that you would be His servant to comfort others."

"But why now? Why am I able to see and speak with you now?"

"I do not know all of what the Almighty will do for you, but He has a message for you."

"A message for me? From the Almighty?" Owen's eyes tried to look into El Bashan's eyes, but he was not able to see clearly because his eyes were blurred with emotion.

After an extended silence, El Bashan spoke again. "Owen, my existence is not as yours. Where I am from, there is no day or night, and time and distance have no relevance. I have not experienced pain, fear, or anxiety as you have, because I was not made from the dust of the earth as you have been. Adonai controls all things, and He is never surprised by the thoughts and actions of human beings. His patience is inestimable and vast, far beyond your understanding. His ways and intentions are beyond your imagination."

But..." was all that Owen could mutter.

"How do you expect to know the mind and intention of the Creator, who spoke planets into existence?"

Again, there was an uncomfortable pause as Owen gathered his emotions. He was not aware of the length of the silence around him.

El Bashan continued. "Adonai created both of us for two purposes, to honour and to serve Him. When the time is right for me to give you the message, I will tell it to you."

El Bashan smiled as Owen's mind recalled past events.

"I have studied the many names of the Almighty," Owen said, "but if you speak with Him, what name do you use?"

"I never speak His name or look at Him when I respond to His words. I was created to listen and not to speak or give an opinion."

The silence that followed was overwhelming. Owen found breathing to be difficult, and words did not form in his mouth. Again, he stared at the floor. After an immeasurable amount of time had passed, Owen asked, "What is heaven like?"

"I have been summoned into all the sanctuaries in the heavens. I have listened to endless songs sung by legions of angels, heard the worship of the archangels and the elders, and experienced the grandeur and magnificence of the Almighty. Earthly language and emotion cannot know or comprehend the magnitude of what exists there. Millions of angelic voices blend and synchronize into sequenced harmony which an earthly ear cannot grasp, comprehend, or appreciate. The sounds of praise offered to the Almighty are something an earthly ear cannot fully absorb."

"I have studied the many names of the Almighty. May I ask which name is used there to speak with him—Adonai, Elohim, or Lord?"

"He is never spoken to by name as you would summon another human. I am His servant. He knows what I need to know, and I know what I must tend to. His will is pure and exceeds all bounds of emotion, reason, and knowledge."

"But..."

El Bashan interrupted. "When the Almighty spoke to Moses in the desert, He referred to Himself as 'I Am That I Am.' His presence is Power as well as Light. His attributes are endless, immeasurable, and difficult to comprehend, and His presence causes man's breathing to cease."

Moments passed as Owen drew a much-needed breath. His mind ceased to function, and words did not flow from his gaping mouth. He remained motionless as he continued to stare without sight.

Several moments later, Owen asked, "What about Yeshua?"

"He is there. His presence and role are part of the essence of the Almighty, which are three in one. His willingness to be sacrificed to redeem sinful humanity is acknowledged and honoured. There is only one Being consisting of three essences: Elohim, the Great I Am, who is the Almighty Father and Creator, the Son Yeshua, and Ru-ach-Ha-Kodesh, the Holy Spirit."

Owen covered his face with both hands. "I am just a man, and there is no health within me. My humanity is..."

"Owen, you are loved by Adonai despite your humanity, which is not a cage or a restriction. Your name is written on the palm of His hand. No one will be able to pluck you from His care."

Immeasurable time passed.

"If you're an angel, is it true there are millions of you?"

El Bashan smiled before speaking. "I do not need to know how many there are, but all have specific duties. There are many who sing, others are warriors to battle evil in spiritual realms, some deliver encouragement, and some are guardians of children, while some generate peace and deliverance. All are messengers who distribute the gospel and perform medical services to humans."

A moment later, a side door into the sanctuary opened. It was Amy. "I'm sorry to disturb you, sir, but Helen has been trying to reach you." She paused. "Sorry, but I didn't know you were speaking with someone." Apologizing, she started to close the door.

"Amy, I'm alright. I've been in here for some time, and I didn't realize it was so late." Owen glanced at his wristwatch as he turned to introduce El Bashan, but El Bashan was not there.

As Amy closed the door and silence returned to the sanctuary, Owen found it hard to breathe, and words did not form in his mouth. His finger tugged at his clerical collar as he stared at the altar, unaware of the time that had elapsed.

Eventually, Owen gathered his thoughts, walked out of the sanctuary, and made his way to his car.

———

Chapter 4
The Hospital Visits

After telephoning Helen, Owen left the church. His drive home was a blur, and when he turned into the driveway, he realized it was almost 6:30 p.m.

Supper was already on the table. Owen said little to Helen or Geo as he mindlessly stirred the contents of the past hours. From habit, he reached for the HP sauce and placed several drops onto his mushy peas before he became aware that Helen was trying to get his attention. He smiled as he replaced the bottle of HP sauce on the table. Helen again tried to engage him in a conversation, but could garner no response.

Geo told him about the soccer practice on Saturday, but Owen continued to rearrange the vegetables on his plate. "Dad, did you hear what I said?"

"I'm sorry, Geo, but I've had a challenging day."

After Owen had eaten supper, he drove to the regional hospital to visit two aged seniors who had been in his congregation for many years.

During his half-hour visit with Eleanor, Owen anointed her forehead with oil and prayed for restoration and healing. He removed the top from a small container of oil, and with his right thumb he made the sign of the cross on her forehead. He prayed, "I anoint you, Eleanor, in the name of the Father, His Son Jesus Christ our Lord, and the Holy Spirit. May He bring healing to your body and grant you peace during this stressful time. Amen."

She gripped his hand. "Thank you, pastor, for your visit and your prayers. I feel peace when you are near. Thank you again."

On the second floor, Owen found Angela sitting in a wheelchair. Around her sat several elderly patients. Some were sleeping, while others appeared confused and dishevelled.

"Good evening, Angela. Tell me about your day," Owen whispered as he touched the top of her head while his eyes scanned the room for a vacant chair.

Angela held a tissue over her mouth as she began to cough uncontrollably. When she had finished, she whispered, "Tomorrow...I begin my...chemotherapy again. Thank you...for coming."

"No need to speak if it's too difficult."

"Thank you for coming," her quivering voice whispered as her breathing continued to produce raspy sounds.

Fifteen minutes later, Owen anointed her forehead with oil and prayed for her. "Lord, grant Angela courage to face these difficult times of uncertainty. May Your peace calm her spirit and ready her for tomorrow," he said as he replaced the container of healing oil into his pocket. As he made the sign of the cross on her forehead, he said, "I anoint you in the name of God our Father, His only begotten Son Jesus Christ our Lord, and the Holy Spirit. May Adonai bring you peace. Amen."

Owen held her fragile hand and allowed her to study his face. He smiled as he rose from his chair and then walked into the hallway.

———

After closing the front door of his home, Owen wiped his shoes on the mat and called to Helen. "I'm home, dear," he said. Then he went into his office to sit at his desk. Eventually, darkness embraced him.

Helen opened the door and whispered, "I've made some tea."

"Thank you, dear. I'll be there in a few moments."

Owen sipped his tea in silence, and Helen understood from his body language and silence that he had experienced a challenging day. When Geo opened the door of the fridge, the light momentarily brought Owen out of deep thought.

"Geo, come over and give me a big hug. I sure need it," Owen said as he extended his arms to embrace the much loved lad.

After Geo had left the kitchen, Helen leaned on Owen's shoulder. "Did you find out who that white-haired man is? Is that why you're so quiet?"

"Yes. I met the man this afternoon in the sanctuary, and I spoke with him."

"You did?" She responded with surprise. "Who is he, and where is he from?"

"Helen, I have not lost my senses, but he told me that he is a servant of the Almighty, so I guess he's an angel sent to..." He nervously stared at his cup while he waited for her response.

Helen studied Owen's face, and though her mouth was open, no words could be heard.

Owen nodded his head up and down. "I know it sounds odd, but..."

"Owen? An angel? Are you sure? How do you know that?"

"I told you. I have spoken to him, and he told me. I have never met anyone like him."

"Did he have wings?" she asked as she tried to lighten the moment.

"No wings, Helen, but I did speak with him."

Helen's eyes studied Owen's facial expression before responding. "What else did he say?"

"He said that he has known me all my life and has a message for me from the Almighty."

"A message? Like what?"

"I'm anxious to find out, but he said I'll have to wait for the proper time to hear it." Owen sat in silence as he rubbed his chin.

"What else has made you so tense?" Helen asked.

Owen continued. "I was in the hospital to visit Eleanor Gibbons and Angela Ringwald. I had prayer with them, but Angela is not doing well. I must return tomorrow."

"Well, it's late, so we should go to bed. We can talk about all of this in the morning."

———————

Chapter 5
The Bazaar

Owen's sleep was restless and constantly interrupted by thoughts of his visit with Eleanor and Angela, but soon his thoughts returned to El Bashan. Somewhere about 3:30 a.m., Owen sat up suddenly and went to the window. He was sure the wind chimes were ringing, but when he parted the drapes, the chimes were silent. After waiting at the bedroom window for some time, he returned to bed and lay down.

At 7:30 a.m., Helen called Owen for breakfast. When he arrived in the kitchen, Geo was walking out the door with his soccer ball.

"I'm off to practice with Danny and Grover, so I'll see yah later, Dad."

"Take care, son," Owen called as Geo closed the door.

"Today is the church bazaar. It looks like a wonderful day," Helen said as she poured fresh coffee into Owen's favourite Father's Day mug. He twisted the corners of his moustache as he stirred his coffee.

An hour later, Owen travelled past the bus stop on Morgan and Hillsborough where he had seen El Bashan. He nervously glanced at six people waiting for the bus. El Bashan was not among them.

After parking in the church parking lot, Owen entered the church gymnasium and watched the ladies who were busy hanging colourful streamers, paper flowers, and knitted bells. There were several dozen tables with knitting, crocheted doilies, books, and fresh cut floral bouquets, as well as tables of baked cookies and cakes.

"Good morning, pastor. This all starts at 10 a.m. Will you be here?" Betty Parry asked. "There are twelve tables with baked goods, some used clothing, gardening tools, toys, and video games for the youth. It will be a wonderful day."

"Ah...yah, I plan to be here," Owen said, then turned and walked down the corridor toward his office.

When Owen returned to the gymnasium, the entrance and lobby were packed with people greeting each other. Owen shook hands with dozens of people who were part of his congregation, as well as with others he recognized as members and adherents of nearby congregations.

Reverend Andrew Adler from Faith Baptist Church hugged him and shook his hand. He greeted Owen with, "The peace of the Lord be with you," and Owen responded, "And also with you."

They chose to sit at a small table nearby and shared cups of coffee and cranberry scones. An hour later, Reverend Adler excused himself and went to the table with baked goods as Owen wandered into the crowd to exchange goodwill.

About 2:00 p.m., Owen was given a bowl of clam chowder, so he sat and ate with several parishioners.

After their conversation concluded, Owen made his way into the sanctuary and knelt at the main altar for prayer. During his time of reflection and prayer, he experienced the familiar feeling that he was being watched, so he lifted his head and looked around. In the back pew sat El Bashan. After making the sign of the cross on his forehead and across his chest, Owen stood and smiled before walking toward El Bashan.

At that moment, a side door to the sanctuary opened. Manny, the verger (custodian), entered and called to Owen, "Sorry to disturb you during your prayers. I didn't know you were in here."

Owen raised his hand and responded, "That's alright, Manny. I was…" He had been about to say something about El Bashan, but when he looked for him, he was no longer there. Owen hurried into the foyer to look for him, but El Bashan was nowhere to be found. Owen returned to the sanctuary and sat in the pew where El Bashan had been.

After sitting there for some time, Owen went into his office and closed the door. He sat in silence before deciding to go home for a rest. He was tired because of the restless night he had had. In the hallway outside his office, he met Mandy Russell, who insisted on telling him about the success of the bazaar. He listened patiently to her and acted as though he was interested.

When he arrived at home, Owen released Freckles from his kennel and then slumped into the hammock on the patio next to the wind chimes. He closed his eyes and listened to their hypnotic melody before falling asleep.

He was surprised when Helen called him for supper. He ate sparingly and then went upstairs and reclined on the bed. Though he reshaped his pillow several times, sleep did not come to Owen because his eyes opened whenever the wind chimes made their hypnotic sound. Eventually, he sat on the edge of the bed. When the grandfather clock rang eight times, he went downstairs to watch the evening news. After a while, Helen insisted that it was Geo's bedtime, so Owen turned off the television but continued to sit in the dimly lit family room. The face of El Bashan flashed before him several times.

Helen entered the room, and as she did, she asked, "What are you fretting about now?"

"I hate to admit it, but I'm distressed knowing that an angel has a message for me. El Bashan's presence has caused me to feel uneasy."

"So, his name is El Bashan?"

"Yes."

"When the time is right, he'll give you the message, so don't borrow from tomorrow to finish this day. Let's go to bed. You need to be rested for tomorrow's Eucharist service."

She came over and placed her arm around Owen's waist as they made their way upstairs together.

———————

Chapter 6
Chaos in a Condo

Opening his unseeing eyes to the darkness around him, Owen reached for the obnoxious sound next to his bed. He was unsure of how many times the telephone had rung before he managed to whisper, "Hello."

A sterile female voice asked, "Is this Owen Richards?"

Owen held the receiver to his ear, and his voice cracked as he responded, "Yes. What do you need?"

The female voice responded in a polite and controlled manner, "Sir, my name is Joan, and I am calling from the 9-1-1 Control Centre. Sergeant Guttridge asked me to call you. We have an incident that might need your expertise. Are you willing to be picked up at your home by an officer?"

"Yes. Yes, I'll be ready in a few moments."

"Let me confirm your home address, sir. 779 Telford Drive, is that correct?"

"Yes."

The dispatcher's voice suddenly became silent as Helen turned on the lamp next to their bed. Owen ran his fingers through his hair as he stood to his feet. Helen reached for his shirt that lay across a chair nearby. Moments later, Owen reached for his socks.

"What was the call about?" asked Helen, as she accompanied him down the staircase to the front door.

"Must be a major disaster. Hope I can be of help," he muttered as he collected his keys from the counter. Helen handed him his cell phone and Bible just before he closed the front door behind him.

Misty darkness covered the neighbourhood as Owen reached for the door handle of the police cruiser. The patrol car backed out of the driveway and then lurched forward as Owen clicked the seatbelt into the closed position. The headlights sprayed light onto bushes and trees as the patrol car swerved around the first corner.

Owen prayed, "God, I have no idea why I am needed, but grant me abilities to do what I have been trained to do. You chose me, so grant me peace."

The officer turned and looked at Owen. "By the way, I'm Constable Ken Allen."

Owen's eyes glanced at the digital clock on the dashboard; it read "1:20."

The officer picked up the microphone. "Dispatch, tell A1 we're on our way."

"Roger."

The vehicle turned several corners and sped along a thoroughfare as it swerved between a few cars that had stopped when the drivers had heard the siren. Ten minutes later, the patrol car turned into a cul-de-sac and stopped next to three police cars parked in front of a luxury condo. The door of the Incident Command Vehicle opened, and Sergeant Guttridge stepped out and approached the patrol car.

"It has been an unbelievable night," Guttridge said. "All EMS vehicles and crews are stretched to the limit, with MVAs, fights, B and Es, domestic calls, suicides, and homicides. I guess this should not be a surprise because it's a full moon."

Owen closed the door of the patrol car and looked at Sergeant Guttridge.

"Sorry, Owen, for bringing you here at this ungodly hour...Ah, sorry for that choice of words, but we have an unusual incident. A young woman destroyed the inside of a condo, and she's out of control. She seems to be on something other than drugs."

Just then, an ambulance arrived, and two paramedics jumped out.

Guttridge raised his hand. "Gentlemen, before you enter the condo, let me tell you about the victim. She's a young woman, about 100 pounds, but she has the strength of two middle linebackers. It took the owner of the condo and three officers to restrain her. We have no idea if she has taken drugs, but she should be taken to a psych ward."

"What else can you tell us about her?" asked one of the paramedics.

"Oh, before you go in, you need to know she claims to be Jesus Christ." Guttridge turned to Owen. "That's why I decided to call you."

After taking a long breath, Owen and both paramedics followed Sergeant Guttridge into the condo. They walked up three steps onto the main floor and into a large room that was a combination dining room/sitting room. Bent and broken lamps were strewn across the floor, along with colourful pillows and an overturned large screen television set. Near the large picture window, an overturned stuffed chair lay across one of the drapes that had been torn from the curtain rod. On the couch sat a small, dark-haired female wearing a torn blouse and blood-soaked sailor pants. Her facial makeup was smeared, and her hair was dishevelled. Her dark, unblinking eyes stared intently at Owen and Sergeant Guttridge as they approached. Three officers stood nearby.

Owen neared the young woman and nodded. She did not nod or smile but continued to stare without blinking her eyes.

"I'm Owen. What is your name?" he asked in an unwavering tone.

She breathed deeply and crossed her tattooed arms.

"What is your name?" asked Owen again.

"I'm Jesus Christ," she muttered.

"Really?" responded Owen.

"I'm Jesus Christ!" she shouted. "If you're a priest, you should know who I am!"

Owen stepped closer as he said, "I believe in Jesus Christ. I speak to Him daily, so I know Him personally."

"Then you should know who I am." She rubbed her arms and then brushed her tinted hair back from her eyes.

"If you are Jesus, can you tell me what happened in this room?"

The restless girl said nothing but sighed deeply. Deep within her, Owen could hear deep moans.

"How can we help you?" asked Owen.

"Why are all of you here?" she asked as she looked down at her hands. Then she slowly turned them over to expose her palms. Her dark, staring eyes glared up at Owen. "What do you want? Why are you here?" she asked.

"Some people are worried about you. By the way, what happened in this room?"

"Don't remember," she whispered. Her voice cracked, and her words became hard to understand.

Both paramedics stood nearby. One of them responded, "We can help you if you are hurt or not feeling well. Is there anything you need?" After a momentary pause, he asked, "Are you a diabetic or taking any medications such as Valium or phenobarbital?"

The young woman turned to the paramedic and shouted, "Get out of my face, you #*&%#&!"

Owen interrupted her outburst. "I told you my name, but you did not tell me your name."

"Are you stupid? I told all of you that my name is Jesus Christ." A moment later she shouted, "I'm Jesus Christ, you #*&%#&!"

"Do you know what time it is?" asked the other paramedic.

She did not answer.

"Do you know where you are?" asked the first paramedic.

She did not answer but breathed deeply as she stared intently at them. The deep guttural moan intensified.

"What is your name?" insisted Owen.

"I have already told all of you. I'm Jesus Christ! Are you hard of hearing, you #*&%#&?"

"May I see your hands?" asked Owen.

She glared at Owen as everyone stared at her hands. She raised both of her arms and turned her hands over slowly to expose the palms.

Owen took both hands, looked down at them, and said, "I don't believe that you're Jesus Christ. He has scars on both hands from His crucifixion. You don't have any scars in your hands. You are a fraud."

Instantly, she jumped to her feet and raised both fists in front of his face. Three officers immediately stepped forward. Within seconds, her strength ebbed, and she slumped to the floor.

As the paramedics escorted her out to the ambulance, Sergeant Guttridge thanked Owen for his willingness to assist. "Here is my card. Call me so I can buy you lunch. This call was more in your league than mine. Thanks, Owen."

"This was certainly different. I'm glad I could help," Owen said, "although I'm not sure I helped much."

Turning to Constable Allen, Sergeant Guttridge said, "Take the padre home."

"Yes, sir."

Neither Allen nor Owen spoke during the ride, but when Owen was reaching for his seatbelt to get ready to leave the patrol car, Allen asked, "Who was the white-haired man in the living room with you when you spoke to that girl? Where did he come from?"

"What white-haired man?"

The officer ran his fingers through his hair as he brought the patrol car to a stop on Owen's driveway. "Who was he, and where did he go? He was there when she stood up, but then he was gone."

Owen was about to exit the patrol car when he heard the police dispatcher call, "1109..."

———————————

Chapter 7
Misfire

Constable Allen responded, "1109. Go ahead."

"Sergeant Guttridge is standing by on channel 5."

"Roger. 1109 on 5 to Alpha 1."

"1109, if the padre is still with you, ask him if he is willing to attend a ninety-nine?"

Constable Allen turned to Owen. "Are you willing to attend an attempted suicide?"

Owen nodded in the affirmative, and Constable Allen responded, "Alpha 1, he has agreed. Have dispatch send me the address."

Moments later the computer screen displayed an address, and immediately the patrol car backed out of Owen's driveway. Soon the red and blue lights began to flash, and the siren was activated.

Dispatch called. "1109, EMS is on their way."

Constable Allen turned onto Melbourne Avenue and increased his speed. Occasionally the patrol car moved into oncoming traffic to avoid getting trapped at an intersection. Owen glanced at the digital clock on the dash. It read, "3:27." After several sharp corners, the officer switched off the siren, and the patrol car slowed to a stop in front of a high-rise apartment complex.

Constable Allen reached for the radio. "1109 is 10-10."

"Roger."

As the officer and Owen entered the lobby of the high-rise, Allen's radio sounded. "1109, come up to the twelfth floor and wait near the vending machines."

"Roger."

On the twelfth floor, another officer motioned Allen to turn down the volume of his radio and wait. Moments later, the elevator door opened again, and two paramedics pushing a stretcher approached the three men standing next to the vending machines.

The officer who had been on the twelfth floor whispered to the EMS personnel, "Turn your radios down."

After about fifteen minutes, the door to the apartment opened, and Sergeant Guttridge stepped out. He motioned for Owen and the two EMS personnel to approach. They stood in the doorway of the apartment.

The sergeant whispered, "We have a roommate talking to the young man in one of the bedrooms. No physical harm has occurred yet, but the subject is sitting in a room with his gun in his lap. We don't know if it's loaded, but things are still very fragile."

"What else should we know about the subject?" asked the female paramedic.

"This is not his first rodeo. We've been here before. This fellow has always been easy to deal with, but this time he brought a gun and three sticks of dynamite into the apartment. Where he got them from is hard to say. Either way, things have escalated since the last time we were here."

"What do we know about him?" asked the paramedic.

"He's in his mid-twenties and is a university student. What triggered him is his failing academic marks, a failed relationship, and the death of his brother in an MVA a week ago."

"Has he been drinking?"

"I suspect so. How much, we don't know."

Owen whispered, "Does he have a priest, a rabbi, or a counsellor?"

"I don't know. That's why we called you. Sorry, padre, for making you work on the Sabbath."

Owen smiled.

A young man emerged from the bedroom and approached Sergeant Guttridge. "He hasn't done anything yet, but he's much the same," the young man said. "I think if someone wearing a uniform goes into the room, he might freak out."

Guttridge suddenly turned and glanced down the hall to where the vending machines were. "Who's the white-haired man standing down there? Does he live in one of these apartments?"

"I happen to know him. He will be no trouble. Leave him be," insisted Owen.

Sergeant Guttridge's stare was as stern as a gunfighter's.

The roommate shrugged his shoulders as he looked at Sergeant Guttridge. "He said he has dynamite, but there's no dynamite that I could see."

"Can I go in?" asked Owen as he turned to Sergeant Guttridge. "And can my white-haired friend join me? He might be of some help."

Guttridge narrowed his gaze before nodding his approval, and Owen motioned for El Bashan to join them.

The roommate led Owen across the living room and into the bedroom. He addressed an unkempt young man sitting on the bed. "Aubrey, these men wish to talk to you, if it's okay with you?"

Two officers and both paramedics remained just outside the bedroom door as Owen entered.

Owen smiled and extended his hand. "I'm Owen. What is your name?"

"I don't remember," came the response as the young man turned his head away.

The roommate responded, "His name is Aubrey."

"Aubrey, I'm Owen."

The dishevelled young man nodded as he wiped tears from his cheeks.

"Do you have any pain?" asked Owen.

"My head hurts, and so does my heart. Everything has gone wrong, and I can't change any of it." Aubrey placed his hands over his eyes. "All I want to do is die."

"What do you know about death?" asked Owen.

"It's quiet, and all pain is gone."

"Who told you that?" Owen sat on the edge of the bed. "What makes you think death is better than life? What if it is worse? How do you get back? Is that gamble worth the great risk?"

Aubrey reached down and picked up a small pistol that had been resting in his lap. He turned it over in his hand and put it to his chin.

"No, Aubrey! Don't do that!" Owen commanded.

The policemen at the door immediately took a step backward and brought their hands down to rest on their service weapons.

As Owen stared at the gun, Aubrey slowly lowered the pistol. Saliva dripped from the corners of his mouth.

"Our intention is not to harm anyone," Owen said, reaching for Aubrey's hand. "That's good. Come with me."

Aubrey closed his eyes, then suddenly raised the pistol to his forehead, and squeezed the trigger twice. Owen took a big breath and reached for the gun that had dropped onto a pillow. The two officers charged into the room, lunged at Aubrey, and wrestled him to the floor.

Sergeant Guttridge appeared at the doorway. "Are you okay, padre?"

"Yes. The pistol misfired. Maybe it wasn't loaded," responded Owen.

Guttridge reached for the pistol and turned it over in his hands. "It was loaded alright, but it misfired. Padre, you were lucky."

After everyone had left the apartment building, Aubrey was driven to the hospital. Owen leaned against the sergeant's vehicle and breathed deeply.

"Well, padre, it's been quite a night, and all you probably wanted was a quiet sleep. Get in, and I'll drive you home. You're lucky that the gun misfired."

Owen wiped his brow as he breathed deeply. "Yes, it's been quite an evening."

Radio discussion between dispatch and other vehicles continued the entire trip to 779 Telford Drive, but otherwise they drove in silence.

"Sorry for such a bad night," Guttridge said again as they pulled into the driveway. "But before you go, I need to ask you. Who was your friend with the white hair, and where did he go? He must have left when we put Aubrey into the ambulance."

"I'll tell you some day when we have the lunch you promised me," Owen said as he closed the door of the patrol car and started up the front steps of his home.

As Owen was about to unlock the front door, it opened, and there stood Helen.

"Welcome home, dear. I was praying for you. You look tired. Come in and have a rest."

———————

Chapter 8
The Eucharist

When Owen arrived at the church Sunday morning, he spoke with Reverend Edward, his associate, and with Deacons Don and Willis.

"Edward, I've had a very trying night and feel exhausted," Owen said. "I'd like to sit in the congregation and leave the entire service to you."

Owen excused himself as he walked down the hallway to the rear of the sanctuary, where Helen met him. The foyer was filled with members, adherents, and guests. Owen and Helen entered the sanctuary and selected a pew near the rear, next to the entrance. Other worshippers hurried in as the organist began to play "A Mighty Fortress Is Our God." A young man carried the Crucifer (cross) down the centre aisle and placed it in its stand near the altar. Edward and the deacons followed, bowing respectfully before the altar and moving to their seats on the stage. Then

Edward stepped to the pulpit and said, "The peace of the Lord be with you." The standing congregation responded, "And also with you."

The rich tones of the pipe organ sounded "Come, Now is the Time to Worship." While the congregation sang, Owen scanned the congregation to see if El Bashan was in the congregation. He saw him seated in the back row on the other side of the sanctuary.

After the congregation finished singing, Edward stepped to the pulpit and read aloud: "Almighty God unto whom all hearts be open, all desires known, and from whom no secrets are hid: cleanse the thoughts of our hearts by the inspiration of Your Holy Spirit, that we may perfectly love You and magnify Your holy Name through Christ our Lord, Amen." Then he led the congregation in the Lord's Prayer.

After a moment of silence, the congregation sat down. Owen found it difficult to concentrate because he was extremely tired and his mind was focused on the message that El Bashan would soon deliver. He tried to determine what the message might be. He relived the cold sound of the misfiring pistol and the screams of the young lady in the condo.

Pastor Edward read the Shema: "Hear, O Israel, the Lord our God, the Lord is one. Love the Lord your God with all your heart and with all your soul and with all your strength. And you shall love your neighbour as yourself. On these two commandments hang all the law and the prophets."

The people responded, "Lord, have mercy upon us and write both these laws in our hearts, we beseech You."

After a momentary pause, Edward said, "Let us stand and declare our faith as we recite the elements of our faith through the Apostles' Creed."

When the congregation had completed reciting the Apostles' Creed, Owen sat down and closed his eyes because of fatigue and the stress of the previous hours.

Helen leaned over and whispered, "Should we go home so you can rest?"

"No, I just need a moment."

"Then I'll go with you to your office so you can lie on the couch."

"Okay, let's go," he whispered as he rose to his feet.

In his office, he reclined on the couch as Helen closed the door. Owen recalled the previous night's activity and the strange conversation with the distraught young female. He recalled Constable Ken Allen's comments about a white-haired man standing next to him during his conversation with the young woman.

"It had to be El Bashan who was there, protecting me," he thought to himself.

Helen reached for his hand because he was mumbling to himself.

Following the service, Edward followed the young man who carried the Crucifer and the altar servers into the foyer. He asked several sidesmen if they knew where Owen had gone, but no one remembered seeing him or Helen. When Edward entered the office, he saw Owen lying on the couch and walked over to him.

Helen reached out to touch Edward's arm. "He had little sleep last night because he was with the police department on several stressful calls."

Owen sat up, even though he felt nauseated. "I'll be alright if I can have something to eat."

Sensing it might be wise to leave the two of them alone to talk, Helen walked out into the hall.

Edward reached for a hanger in his closet to hang up his frock. "I saw you leave the sanctuary. Are you sure you feel alright?"

Owen walked over to the door of the office and closed it. "Have a seat, Edward," he said as he opened his hand to point at the couch. Then he told Edward about the white-haired visitor in his backyard and about seeing him at the bus stop, in front of the Tim Horton's coffee shop, and in the sanctuary during his prayers.

"Last night, I was called to a distressing call with the police department, to assist a mentally confused female who claimed to be Jesus Christ. Afterwards, a police officer asked me about a white-haired man who was standing next to me. Later, I was asked to speak with a university student who intended to commit suicide. He tried to kill himself, but the gun misfired, and again the white-haired man was in the room with me." He paused. "I got home about six a.m."

"Who is this man?" asked Edward as he rubbed his chin. He stared at Owen and waited for a response.

"I've spoken to him, and he said his name is El Bashan. He told me that he is a servant of the Almighty, a messenger sent by Adonai, so I guess that makes him an angel."

There was an uncomfortable silence as Edward cast his eyes to the floor. "Owen, are you sure?"

"El Bashan spoke with me when I was in the sanctuary praying." Owen brushed his hair with the palm of his right hand. "And he was in the sanctuary today."

"I don't remember seeing a white-haired man sitting in the sanctuary. As I recall, only the Cranston and Cleveland families were seated next to you and Helen."

Owen reached for his Bible, turned to Hebrews 13, and read the first two verses: "Keep on loving one another as brothers and sisters. Do not forget to show hospitality to strangers, for by so doing some people have shown hospitality to angels without knowing it."

"Owen, I don't know what to say. Why is this event such an issue with you? If this man is an angel sent by God, why are you fearful of him?"

"But why me?" Owen asked as he raised his shoulders slightly. "He told me he has been my guardian all my life."

"If God has a message for you, Owen, and this angel fellow has been sent to deliver it, you will know soon enough. I'll keep my eyes open for him. If I see him, I'll let you know," Edward said. "Owen, your heavenly Father means you no harm, so wait. In due time, you will know what this is all about. You are usually a patient man, so relax. Everything will be alright."

There was an extended pause as silence descended on the room.

"It has been a trying morning. What else will cross my path?" Owen asked after a time.

Just then, there was the sound of a siren nearing the church. It became increasingly louder until it suddenly stopped when it reached the church. Loud voices could be heard.

Owen and Edward walked rapidly toward the entrance doors. Outside, two paramedics were kneeling by someone who was lying on the roadway in front of the parking lot. A firetruck arrived moments later, and several firefighters stepped from the truck to assist the paramedics.

The small crowd parted when Owen and Edward arrived and began pushing their way to the centre of the activity. Owen's eyes widened as he stared at a young lad lying prostrate in front of a vehicle.

A voice called out, "Pastor Owen! It's Geo!"

A paramedic searched for a carotid pulse as the second paramedic controlled the hemorrhaging to Geo's face. Firefighters brought the stretcher to their side while a paramedic inserted an oropharyngeal airway between Geo's blood-stained lips. Moments later, a firefighter handed the paramedic a mechanical ventilator known as a bag valve mask.

Owen heard someone say, "Geo and several of his friends were running after the soccer ball when it bounced into the street, and that is when Geo was struck by the vehicle."

Owen could take in little of what he was hearing and seeing. He looked down at the blood on Geo's clothes and then up at the bewildered faces around him. His eyes widened as he saw El Bashan kneeling next to Geo.

Owen knelt next to Geo and touched him, wanting to gather him up in his arms, but the firefighters encouraged him to step aside. A paramedic placed a cervical collar around Geo's neck, and then the paramedics carefully placed Geo on the stretcher and moved him to the rear of the ambulance. Moments later, a police car arrived just as the ambulance started for the regional hospital.

Owen stood to his feet as he wiped his bloodied hands on his shirt. An elderly woman who stood nearby collapsed, and some members began attending to her. Edward placed his arm around Owen's shoulders and then quietly asked some of the onlookers to enter the sanctuary to pray for Geo, Helen, and Owen.

In total confusion and anguish, Owen stared at all that was happening around him but saw nothing. His mind tried to understand what had just happened but failed.

Chapter 9
O My Son Geo, O Geo My Son

Owen remembered little about the trip to the hospital. Deacon Don drove him and accompanied him to the Emergency Room, where they found two nurses and two doctors attending to Geo. Eventually, a nurse escorted Owen and Don to a family quiet room, where they were asked to wait.

"This quiet place allows families to grieve away from the public. When other family members arrive, we will usher them into this room to be with you," the nurse said as she quietly shut the door.

Don volunteered to find a coffee shop in the hospital. When Don left the room, Owen turned to face a large window where the sun's warm rays were flooding in. In silence, he dabbed tears from his eyes and cheeks.

A clerk opened the door and said in a quiet voice, "Your wife is on her way, sir, and she should be here shortly."

Owen closed his eyes as he searched his pockets for more tissues. When he was able to focus on his reflection in the window again, he realized that El Bashan was standing behind him. He turned to speak to El Bashan, but he was not there. Owen looked back at the reflection in the window.

"El Bashan! Are you here? I know you are. We desperately need you."

Owen felt a hand on his shoulder. "The Almighty wants you to know..." whispered El Bashan.

"But, El Bashan, this is my only son, and the pain is so great. I don't think we can go on without him. I feel so empty." Owen covered his face with both hands as he fell into a chair.

"The Almighty was also distressed when His only Son was put to death. He turned His face away because the pain was so great. The Almighty knows the pain you are experiencing."

"But, El Bashan..."

Just then, the door to the quiet room opened, and Helen stepped in. With tears streaming down her cheeks, she rushed toward Owen, her arms reaching for him. He stood and embraced her.

"Owen. Owen, is Geo alright? Have you seen him?"

"I don't know how he is because I've been in here for some time and they haven't spoken to me." He held Helen tightly.

Several painful minutes passed before Owen glanced at the reflection in the window. When he did, he saw El Bashan standing behind them. The situation seemed unreal.

Don stepped into the room with two coffees. "Owen, here's a coffee for you and one for Helen."

"Thank you, Don, but I'm unable to drink anything right now, so please keep it for yourself."

"What about Helen?"

She shook her head and whispered, "No thanks, Don."

Owen felt compelled to kneel next to the small couch, where he began to pray. "Almighty God, with You there are no surprises, and You see everything from the beginning to the ultimate outcome. What we need now is...the ability to accept the outcome because we know it will be within Your will."

Helen's deep moans were punctuated with loud, intermittent sobs.

As Owen stood to his feet, he felt drained of all strength. Time stood still. There was no place of comfort.

The quiet room door opened again, and a physician in blue scrubs entered the room. "I am Dr. Nancy Sahota, the Chief Casualty Officer on duty. We transferred your son to the surgical suite, but there was little we could do. It is never easy to bring this kind of news to grieving parents. I'm so sorry."

Helen moaned loudly when she comprehended the devastating news.

"May we see him?" asked Owen, his voice quivering.

"I understand why it is important for you, but until the trauma team have had time to prepare your son for viewing, I can't let you see him. I'm sorry for your loss."

"What do we do now?"

"I expect the hospital chaplain will be by in the next few minutes," Dr. Sahota said as she placed her hand on the doorknob. "Sorry, but I have other trauma patients to attend to."

She left the room, and silence surrounded them. Owen turned to stare at the reflection in the window, and there in the reflection stood El Bashan.

"El Bashan, we need your help. Now what?" His arms were extended as far apart as possible. His pain seemed to drain his very soul.

During the silence that followed, Don moved next to Owen and whispered, "Who is Elbash?"

"He's an angel I've met and talked to."

"An angel?" Don questioned as his eyes narrowed. "Is he here? Has this Elbash fellow been here all along, and have you talked with him before?" He tilted his head to one side as his eyes studied Owen's face.

Owen silently nodded in the affirmative.

"Well, ask him why he didn't intervene," Don demanded.

"He told me that he does only what he is told to do and he makes no decisions on his own. He is only a servant."

"An angel? Huh," responded Don, sounding skeptical.

Some time later, Dr. Steve Kramer entered the quiet room and walked up to Owen. "Owen, was that your son in the ER who was transferred to the surgical suite?"

"Yes, and I was notified that he has passed away," Owen responded. He swallowed as he wiped his eyes with damp tissues.

Helen sobbed loudly as she clung to Owen.

"Owen, you should probably change your clothes," Dr. Kramer said, pointing to the blood-stained shirt Owen was wearing.

"Yes. I need to wash my hands," Owen whispered as he looked down at Geo's blood on his quivering hands.

But Owen was unable to enter the washroom to wash his hands because Helen was clinging so tightly to him. Her sobs were loud and painful.

"How long will we have to wait before we get to see Geo?" Owen asked.

Dr. Kramer volunteered to speak to the nursing staff, but when he returned, he informed them that they would have to call the coroner's office in the morning because of hospital protocol. "Owen, if you need to talk with someone this evening, call me. My shift ends at midnight. Here is my home telephone number and my cell number." Dr. Kramer patted Owen on the shoulder as he left the room.

"Thank you, doctor."

Turning to Don, Owen said quietly, "Don, will you drive us home? There is nothing we can do here. We want to be alone."

"Okay," Don responded.

Out in the parking lot, Don felt compelled to ask, "Owen, who is this Elbash guy? Is he really an angel person that you talked to? Where is he now? What does he look like?"

"Yes, Don. He is real, but I'm not sure how to explain what he looks like."

———————

Chapter 10
Grieving Is Empty Loneliness

The evening at home was painful and merciless. There was no place of comfort, no way of escape from their relentless agony. The silence accentuated Helen and Owen's emptiness. Even Freckles seemed to mourn as he shuffled from room to room looking for Geo. He seemed to sense that all was not well in the Richards home.

When darkness claimed the neighbourhood, Helen reclined on the couch and swaddled herself in a colourful knitted shawl, which muffled her small gasps and weak cries. Overwhelmed by the events of the day, she stared into the darkness as hundreds of memories flooded her shattered mind. About ten o'clock, Freckles lay down beside her, closed his eyes, and fell into a troublesome sleep. Often, he whimpered, moaned, and sighed. Helen stirred when the grandfather clock chimed its quarterly cadence. She adjusted the shawl around her shoulders.

Owen stepped onto the patio and slumped into his favourite padded chair, in the hope that he could find some comfort. Leaning back, he thought of the changes that had come into their lives. When a breeze caused the chimes to gently ring, Owen instantly glanced up at them and then looked at the bench next to the pathway that led to the coy pond. Hearing a squeak from one of the patio chairs next to him, he turned, and there sat El Bashan. He neither smiled nor frowned but remained perfectly still.

Neither spoke as the wind chimes pinged from a gentle breeze.

Owen whispered, "I have the feeling you've been here all along."

El Bashan nodded in the affirmative, but said nothing.

Ten minutes passed before El Bashan spoke. "What happened today was no one's fault. Sadness and pain are the result of mankind's disobedience in Eden. Godlessness and evil exist in every generation and culture. Job lost his sons and daughters when a strong wind came from the wilderness and collapsed the building they were in. Other nations have had many of their citizens murdered, and the only reasons were hatred, jealousy, and greed. I have been told to tell you that no one is to blame for this painful experience. Take comfort in knowing that Geo's spirit is safe in the care of the Almighty. Read what is written in Psalm 116:15."

Owen sat with his eyes closed and listened to the sporadic traffic passing his home. "Why is death so painful?" he whispered.

"The Almighty's Son has destroyed the intimidation of death. It no longer has power over a believer, but it is a method to safely remove believers from this earth so that they may enter Paradise. Psalm 116:15 tells us: 'Precious in the sight of the Lord is the death of his faithful servants.'"

"Could all of this have been avoided? Was Geo destined to have this accident?" Owen ran his fingers through his hair, leaving it poking out in several directions, a sign of his deep distress.

After a pause, El Bashan said, "In your language, the word 'destined' is often given inerrant overtones. Some people have propagated the idea that what is predestined is inevitable, something that cannot be altered except by the Almighty. Many people live their lives with the concept that everything that happens is beyond their control and is determined by fate. In their minds, 'fate' and 'predestined' are interchangeable. However, the Almighty has granted people freedom of choice. Believing that fate has power equal to that of my Master is dangerous and untrue and is a form of idolatry. Fate does not exist, for it has no power, accountability, or responsibility."

"But was Geo's accident destined to occur?"

"Geo was granted choices, and some choices are morally neither good nor bad. Our Master is not accountable to anyone. Events frequently occur which have results which are less than desirable."

Owen sighed loudly as he closed his eyes. "It is hard to see any good in this painful tragedy, and I am not ready to accept it just yet. I'm too upset."

"When Job's children died when the house collapsed on them, that event was extremely painful. Job mourned as you are mourning now. It certainly does not mean that the Almighty is pleased with what has happened, but, as a pastor and priest, you should know that you and Helen will be granted peace and comfort to soothe your spirits. My Master takes no pleasure in your sorrow. He will grant you peace. It may make little sense at this moment, but thank Him for allowing you to enjoy the years you had with Geo. Your faith will grow whenever you thank Him."

Moments later, Helen stepped onto the patio. "I heard voices. Who were you speaking with?"

Owen turned to look at El Bashan, but he was no longer there.

"Owen, please come inside and sit with me," she whispered as she reached for Owen's hand.

Several times, telephone calls interrupted their intense grieving. Owen allowed the answering machine to record the well-meaning messages sent by concerned parishioners.

At midnight, the doorbell rang, and Freckles ran to the front door and began to bark. There stood Owen's assistant Edward and Deacon Don. They hugged and prayed together in the entryway, attempting to comfort Owen.

Five days later, the sanctuary was crowded with relatives from nearby cities and distant places, as well as church members and adherents from Owen's church and nearby churches. The stage and the casket were covered with floral displays and banners with the name "Geo." There were dozens of colourful photographs of Geo in infancy, at school, and at community soccer games. In the front row of the sanctuary sat a dozen young boys in their soccer uniforms.

Following the memorial, family members met in Castle Hill Cemetery. When the short internment service was complete, the church family returned to the church gymnasium, where friends shared encouragement, fellowship, and refreshments. Though the atmosphere was friendly and the presence of so many people was comforting, there lingered the scent of deep pain.

When the grandfather clock bonged twelve times, Owen reached over and squeezed Helen's hand. She smiled, and Owen watched as her smile faded in the dim light of the porch light.

He closed his eyes and breathed deeply while his mind relived the tragedy of Geo's death. Many things rushed through his mind—recitals, sporting events at school, soccer games, and church picnics.

He heard the wind chimes gently ringing, so he opened his eyes. Surprised that Helen was not there, he lifted his head to see El Bashan sitting in the lounge chair where Helen had been seated.

"El Bashan, is that you?"

"Helen went to bed some time ago. I know you have had a trying day, but it is now two-thirty, and you should get your rest."

"El Bashan, everything is in chaos. My mind is unable to comprehend everything that is happening. I doubt I will be able to function again. Do you have advice for me?"

"My task is not to provide advice but to protect you. If Adonai wishes me to bring a message to you, then I will. Remember that Adonai will provide whatever you need."

"What about tomorrow and the day after that?"

"Owen, I do not see the future, nor do I provide advice. Remember that I am only a servant, as you are."

After El Bashan had departed, Owen continued to sit on the porch. Tears washed his cheeks as his grief overwhelmed him. His heart felt broken, and deep sobs made his chest ache. Finally, he rose and shuffled into the house to try to get some rest.

———————

Chapter 11
An Interesting Guest

An echoing emptiness was all that was left in the hearts of Helen and Owen, while their minds constantly roiled and swelled with endless memories. They were unable to find any comfort. Happiness had eluded their home, and seclusion was all Helen desired. Had it not been for Owen's disciplined prayer life, he might have succumbed to permanent sadness and depression.

During his prayer time on the patio, the wind chimes tinkled their hypnotic tone. Owen immediately paused, opened his eyes, and turned to stare at the patio chair next to the chimes.

"El Bashan, is that you?" whispered Owen.

"I have been next to you and Helen during all of these difficult days."

"El Bashan, our pain is so great..."

"Yes, Adonai is aware of your pain and ordeal. He wants you to know that both of you are loved.

Your name is etched on the palm of His hand, and no one can pluck you from His care."

"I'm so glad you have returned," responded Owen.

"Do not cling to me, Owen, for I am not your God. I am only a servant. Your focus must be on Jesus."

"El Bashan..."

"I did not go away. Adonai wants you to accept these events so your faith can mature during this trial. You will grow in strength and have more empathy toward others."

Owen closed his eyes and sighed loudly.

"Owen, Adonai has arranged for a guest to meet you. He will encourage you and bring a blessing to you. This person has experienced what you and Helen have experienced, and he will deliver what Adonai desires for you. Do not fear when he appears but embrace what Adonai sends to you."

———————

Several days later, Owen decided to return to his office because Amy had called about someone who wanted to speak with him.

"He's called every day and has dropped into the office twice, so I thought I'd better call you," she said.

"Fine. I'll be in tomorrow. Who, is he?"

"He said his name is Rabbi Herschel Lachman."

"A rabbi wants to see me?"

"Yes. He said he'd be here tomorrow afternoon."

When Owen entered the church office, Amy leaped to her feet, extended her arms, and shouted, "Pastor Owen, it is so good to see you!"

Owen stepped next to her and hugged her.

"Do I have any urgent appointments or issues to attend to other than this rabbi?" he asked.

"No. Everything has been taken care of. Reverend Edward and the deacons have been busy handling visits, counselling, and office duties. Will you be here long?"

"No. I just dropped by to see if there were any urgent issues or messages—and to meet this rabbi."

"Returning to her desk, Amy picked up several message slips. "The only urgent one is from Rabbi Lachman. He seems very anxious to speak with you. He claims to be a Messianic rabbi. He left his telephone number."

Taking the message slips, Owen slowly walked into his office as he mumbled to himself, "I don't know a Rabbi Lachman."

After taking off his coat, he sat in his office chair, leaned back, and sighed.

At the door, Amy asked, "If calls come in for you, do you wish for me to take a message or shall I forward them to you?"

"Take messages for now, but first I need to have a few moments."

Entering the sanctuary, Owen stepped to the altar rail before kneeling to pray. His mind flashed back to the day he had first met El Bashan. After a few moments, he made the sign of the cross across his chest and began to pray. "Father God, the last days have been extremely difficult. Restore the joy of my salvation and renew my spirit. Grant me peace."

Owen felt a hand on his shoulder, so he turned. There, kneeling beside him, was El Bashan.

"El Bashan..."

"Speak with Adonai, not me. Remember that I am only a servant."

"Most Holy God, my trust is in You. I will try not to be afraid. If You are with me, I will renew my commitment to You."

Some time later, after Owen had returned to his office, Amy appeared at his office door. "Sorry to interrupt you. Rabbi Lachman is here to see you."

"Well, usher him in."

At the door stood a short, rotund, elderly man wearing a black suit. On his head, he wore a kippah. His beard parted to display a warm smile and shiny white teeth. Owen stood to his feet as the rabbi extended his hand.

"Shalom, Mr. Minister Owen. I am Rabbi Lachman."

"Please have a seat," said Owen, his open hand directing the rabbi to a padded chair near the window.

"Tank you varry much. I have come, not by invitation, but by vanting to meet you. I, too, have lost a son, so I know of da struggles inside of you. It feels like someone fighting inside me, but I don't know how to stop him."

"Yes, it is a struggle."

"Do you have any odder children?"

"No."

"It matters not how many you have. Whether you have six or more, losing a son is not easy. I still have six—four boys and two girls. Von of my boys vas lost while swimming at da lake. Dese children are all of great value to me, and I vould not sell any von of dem for a million dollars. But…" His eyes closed, and his head moved from side as he raised a pointed finger. "To tell you da truth, I vould not buy another von for fifty cents."

Amy appeared at the door. "Could I offer you something to drink, rabbi?"

"Ah. No, tank you."

Turning to Owen, the rabbi continued. "Vere vas I? Oh, yah, the loss of your son. Someting told me to come by and comfort you. We may have different families, but both of us worship Adonai, the God of Abraham, Isaac, and Jacob. We also believe that Yeshua is the only Son of God, yes? God's Son died too, as you know, so Adonai knows about pain too."

"How did you find out about my son?"

"The synagogue I serve is not far from here. I read about it in da newspaper."

"My wife and I are struggling," Owen admitted, "but Adonai, is comforting us."

"Nonbelievers refuse to tink about death and vat happens after dat. Dey tink it is the end, but if you tink about it, it is only da start, da beginning of much more. Your son is in Adonai's hand, and your life is different and new. Yeshua raised Lazarus, and He raised Jairus's daughter, and He vas able to be raised Himself. So, your son and my son vill also be raised."

"Thank you for your encouragement," Owen responded.

"Yeshua vill raise both our sons. My son's name was Ehud."

"Ehud?"

"Yes, he vas a good son, he vas not to blame for dying, but tings change quickly." The rabbi raised his finger as he continued. "Do not despair, because despair is lack of faith. You are a man of faith, so believe." His smile displayed his white teeth.

"Thank you."

"I phoned you many times, but you vere always away, so I tought I vould come by today because I vas driving by anyway, so here I am."

Owen nodded and said again, "Thank you."

"I must admit dis is da first time I have been to a gentile rabbi's office place." His head turned slowly as his eyes scanned the books in Owen's library. After a few moments of silence, Rabbi Lachman cleared his throat and said, "I have always heard dat time heals, but it is Adonai who heals, not time. Be sad, but remember dat people are watching you in your grief, so don't make dem tink Adonai has abandoned you."

"And what can I do for you?" asked Owen.

"I did not come here to get someting from you, but to tell you dat pain is a great equalizer. Nothing surprises Adonai, and He takes no pleasure in your pain, but Adonai seeks your need of Him. You exist because He exists. I will say the Aaronic blessing over you, to bring you Shalom."

Owen closed his eyes as Rabbi Lachman stood to his feet, raised both hands, spread his fingers, and began to pray in Hebrew. Then he spoke in English, in a strong voice: "The Lord bless you and keep you; the Lord make His face shine on you and be gracious to you; the Lord turn His face toward you and give you Shalom."

Owen dabbed his eyes with tissues as Rabbi Lachman ended his blessing.

"Before I leave, I have von qvestion. Who vas dat white-haired man in da hallvay? Is he your friend?"

"Ah, yes."

"Vat is his name?"

"El Bashan."

"He sounds Jewish."

"Well, yes, he does."

"Vere does he come from?"

Owen hesitated. "Heaven."

"Heaven? How can dat be? Is he an angel?"

There was an extended pause before Owen responded. "Yes. As a matter of fact, yes."

"Gentiles have angels?"

Owen nodded.

"Dat's da problem with angels. Now you see dem and den dey're gone."

They shook hands. Before turning to leave, Rabbi Lachman said, "Adonai has sent me to encourage you during your grief. Shalom."

After Rabbi Lachman had left, Amy peered around the open office door and looked at Owen, who now was sitting in silence.

"Are you alright?" she asked.

Owen did not respond or move.

"I heard you talking. Is that white-haired man you mentioned a real angel? Is he from God?"

"If this gets out, many people will be afraid," suggested Manny, the verger, who was standing in the hallway.

"There is nothing to fear. God sent him, he is my protector, and he has been here for many years. It's just that few have seen or spoken to him."

"If he is your protector, where was he when Geo was injured?" Amy asked.

"He is a servant of the Most High and does only what he is told to do and says only what he is told to say. My life is in God's hands, not his. If you see him, don't be afraid. He will not harm you."

"Pastor Owen, does Pastor Edward know about this?" Amy asked.

"Yes, and now you both know."

Amy rubbed her arms as she said, "I have chills thinking about this."

———

Chapter 12
The Church Council Meeting

When the monthly meeting of the church council was about to conclude, chairperson Phillip Graham announced, "There is one more item to discuss and to formally approve. The item is not listed on the agenda, but it has been approved in principle by everyone sitting at this table—except our rector, Owen Richards."

Owen raised his gaze to include all the council members around the oval table. "I'm sorry, Chairman Graham. I do not understand," he said.

"Owen, we as board members are aware that your vacation time is near, but we are recommending that you accept a three-month sabbatical to be added to your vacation time. It will be a sabbatical with full wages, which will allow you and Helen to travel and have an extended vacation. It is hoped that this time will bring healing to both of you."

"Thank you for your kindness. I know Helen will appreciate this generous offer, and I...I don't know what to say. But thank you."

When Owen arrived home, he explained the generosity being extended to them by the council. Helen was shocked by the news and expressed her delight by hugging Owen.

A week passed as Helen visited travel agencies for brochures. Amy telephoned several churches to see if any of their clergy might be interested in caring for Owen and Helen's home while they were out of the country. Amy found a youth pastor and his family from another denomination to reside in their house while they were on their planned vacation to Europe.

Before starting their vacation, Owen applied for teaching positions in several Anglican seminaries in England and made plans to visit them while on their vacation.

Their itinerary included visits to Buckingham Palace, St. Paul's Cathedral, Lambeth Palace, Hampton Court Palace, and the Tower Bridge. Additional plans included a trip to France via the Eurotunnel, which runs beneath the English Channel between Folkestone, England, and Coquelles, France.

As their 747 sat at the end of the runway, Owen noticed a white-haired head several rows ahead of them.

"El Bashan," whispered Owen.

As the engines began to roar, Helen leaned over and asked, "Did you say something, dear?"

Moments later, the plane began its ascent, but Owen could not take his eyes off the white-haired head in row 5, seat C.

During the flight, once the fasten seatbelt sign had been turned off, Owen walked toward the white-haired head at the front of the plane. When he got there, he leaned forward and whispered, "El Bashan?"

The lady who was in the seat next to where El Bashan had been seen looked at Owen. "Can I help you?"

"I thought there was a man seated next to you. Sorry."

"This seat has been empty."

Owen excused himself and returned to his seat.

When Owen and Helen disembarked at Heathrow Airport, El Bashan was nowhere to be seen, so they gathered their luggage and found a cab.

During their first week, Owen visited several Anglican seminaries. However, after several informal interviews and enquiries, he found he was unhappy with the liberal teachings, philosophies, and interpretations of the scriptures there, so he turned down all offers.

Ten days later, they arrived in Paris, where they were scheduled to view the Eiffel Tower and the Louvre museum. Their itinerary was interrupted when Owen unexpectedly became quite ill. Additional plans to visit Italy and Israel were set aside, and they decided to return to Canada. Upon their arrival in Canada, Helen arranged an appointment for Owen to see Dr. Kramer.

After assessing Owen's vital signs, Dr. Kramer asked him, "What symptoms did you experience while in Europe?"

"Nausea, extreme weakness, and some mild shortness of breath," responded Owen, "but I feel well now. And, oh, both hands were extremely itchy. They felt as if something inside was gnawing on my muscles. I was constantly scratching them, and the only thing that stopped it was when I ran cold water over them."

"Go on."

"I even used a hairbrush to scratch them."

"Any angina or heart palpitations?"

"Occasionally. Mild."

"What did you do to alleviate the pain and discomfort?"

"ASA seemed to help, and when I rested, the pain seemed to ease."

"Were you treated by any physicians in England or France?"

"No."

"Well, I am going to order a series of blood tests, an EKG, and an angiogram. I want you to remain in the hospital during this series of tests. I will arrange for oxygen therapy and a nitroglycerin spray, as well as an echocardiogram. Dr. Laurant, a renowned cardiologist, will be your caregiver there. I know him well and respect his knowledge and thoroughness."

———————

Two weeks later, Dr. Kramer and Dr. Laurant met at Owen's bedside. They recommended that several stents be inserted into two cardiac arteries to improve the blood flow to Owen's heart.

An hour before the medical procedure was scheduled, El Bashan appeared to Owen. "Owen, there is no reason to fear. Adonai wants you to trust Him more than you trust those who will treat you."

Fourteen days later, Owen was released from the hospital with numerous medications and a list of future appointments.

Few noticed, but Owen's hair gradually turned grey over the next few months. From above, his haircut resembled that of Friar Tuck because a small, shiny balding spot was now present behind his thinning hairline.

———————

Chapter 13
Feeling the Fear

Over the following eleven months, Owen gradually returned to his regular duties at the church. His regular walks strengthened him, and he was careful to watch his diet and take his medications. More time passed. He preached often and maintained a busy schedule, including visiting parishioners who were in hospital.

After having prayer with an octogenarian and also a young woman who had just given birth to twins, Owen started down the hallway. When he neared the elevator, he recognized El Bashan standing next to the entrance of a room. El Bashan smiled and pointed into the room before disappearing.

Owen entered the room and saw a man with a large cast on his leg lying on a bed and another man standing next to a window. Bright sunlight was shining on this second man as he breathed deeply.

Owen neared the man standing in the sunshine and said, "Warm sunlight seems to penetrate the body, and it may assist in healing."

The man turned and narrowed his gaze. "You look like the padre who assisted me a few times some years ago. Yes, I remember you. I promised you a breakfast, but you never dropped by the station."

"Are you Sergeant Guttridge?" asked Owen.

"Yes, I am. I thought of you earlier today when I saw your white-haired friend standing in the hallway. We never spoke, but he smiled at me."

"Why are you here?"

"I've been diagnosed with prostate cancer and pancreatic cancer. The odds of surviving prostate cancer may be 50-50, but the odds of surviving pancreatic cancer are essentially zero."

"I'm sorry to hear that."

"That's why I'm standing in the bright, warm sunshine because I hear that it's dark and cold in a casket."

After a long pause, Sergeant Guttridge sat in a chair next to the window. Owen sat in another chair facing him.

"You know, padre," Guttridge said after a while. "I've been shot at, been threatened with butcher knives, been in many barroom brawls, and fought Hells Angels, but dammit—sorry, padre—I've always been able to fight all of them with my fists. This one...well, this one I don't think I'll win."

Owen sat in silence as the sergeant sighed loudly.

"I can't put on a bulletproof vest or fight back. I can feel the enemy, but I can't see him. It frustrates me. If only I could grab the..." He moved the palm of his hand across his face.

"Please call me Owen."

"I'm Angelo, but you can call me Ange."

Owen adjusted his position in the chair.

"Padre—I mean Owen—I feel so helpless, like I'm skiing down a mountain and I've never skied in my life. This is going to be a train wreck. What do you suggest?"

"It sounds to me that you have experienced real fear for the first time. You don't have control."

"You have that right, Owen. For the first time in my life, I know what fear is, and I don't like it."

"Fear is an emotion. We all experience fear at some time in our life. Your fear is of the future.

Knowing what is coming is stressful. Often what people fear most is dying."

Guttridge groaned as he stood to his feet. "All these years I never thought about dying. Is there any way to prepare for it?" His eyes stared at a spot on the wall.

"Ange, when you need to have your car fixed, you go to a mechanic. When a tooth hurts, you go to a dentist. So, if you want peace about dying, you speak to God. I am not God, but I know Him and am willing to speak to Him for you."

Ange returned to his seat. "Keep talking. I'm listening."

"God sent His Son, Jesus, to earth to rescue people like you and me. He knows how weak and hopeless we are, so He made it simple. He knows people can't follow all the rules, so they won't be able to avoid death and earn a chance to live forever. Jesus came to earth and was killed, sacrificed for our sins, for the things we have done wrong. But then He was resurrected—He came back to life, and in doing so He defeated death."

"Is that what churches celebrate at the holiday called Easter?"

"Yes. God has made it easy for us to live forever. All we need to do is believe Jesus is the

Son of God, confess our sins to Him, and put our trust in Him."

"It's that easy? When can I do that?"

"You can do it right now."

"That's great, padre. I don't think I have much time!"

"Praying is just like talking, having a conversation with God. You can speak to him now, from your heart."

"Okay, padre. How's this?" the sergeant said. "Jesus, this is Ange Guttridge. Please save me and let me live forever. Um, Owen told me about You. I hope that's okay."

The two men spoke late into the evening. Owen prayed with Guttridge and gave him a New Testament.

"Ange, read this section. It's called the Gospel of John. I may not be able to be here tomorrow, but I will be back. Have a peaceful night."

They shook hands before Owen left the room.

The next afternoon, Owen arrived at the hospital to visit Don Alexander, a ninety-five-year-old member of the church. Afterward, he stopped by Guttridge's room and was surprised to see a young man in the bed next to the window.

He approached the nursing station. "Where is Ange Guttridge? Have they released him?" he asked.

Taking note of Owen's clerical collar, the nurse said, "I'm sorry, but Mr. Guttridge passed away during the night."

———

At the memorial service at the funeral home, nineteen uniformed officers followed the casket into the parlour. Soft music played as the casket was put into place, surrounded by several bouquets of flowers. Only six other people attended the service.

———

Chapter 14
The New Challenge

At the annual synod meeting in Toronto, Owen was nominated to become an area bishop for the province of Alberta. The recent growth in church attendance and successful church planting efforts had created a need for additional oversight. Owen and Helen had been consulted prior to the synod meeting, and after much discussion and prayer, they had decided to accept the new challenge.

Stopping in Alberta on the way home from Toronto, Owen and Helen spent a week with a realtor and eventually purchased a home in the Wildwood neighbourhood of Calgary. After spending the next few weeks packing their possessions and selling their home, they prepared for the moving van to come to pick up their possessions.

Before leaving for their new assignment, Helen made one final visit to Geo's graveside. She wept next to the headstone and lingered for hours before getting back into her vehicle to drive home. She was finally ready to let go. Qualified grief counsellors had helped her to return to her former optimistic lifestyle. Working through the book *75 Bible Verses to Comfort You Through Hard Times* by Verna May had also helped. Prayers offered by friends and parishioners had been greatly appreciated and had helped her to adjust.

The change of scenery, new challenges and opportunities, and a busy schedule in Alberta also helped with healing. Years passed as Owen continued to do effective ministry, offering wise counsel and a comforting presence to many people. Helen also found new ways to be involved and bless others.

Whenever Owen felt heaviness from the memory of Geo, he would sit in his favourite reclining chair on the patio overlooking the Bow Valley. Then, one afternoon while he was reading, a breeze softly touched the wind chimes on his patio. Owen immediately held his breath and glanced up at them. His heart quickened, for he had not heard them ringing for several days.

"El Bashan, is that you?"

An extended silence followed.

"El Bashan, is that you? Are you here?" Owen whispered again. "I would like to talk with you."

"I've been here all along," Owen heard El Bashan say. "Adonai has not abandoned you and Helen. He wants you to know that He loves both of you very much. You are His, and no one can pluck either of you from His hand."

The book in Owen's hand closed slowly and silently slid to the ground. "El Bashan, I've not seen or spoken to you for a long time. I was fearful that you would not return."

"I have been near you all along. You may not have seen me, but I have been nearby. Who do you think kept you from that highway off-ramp accident on the Deerfoot Trail? My Master will never abandon you, and neither will I."

"El Bashan, what is the message that you were sent to deliver?"

El Bashan sat down in a chair next to Owen as he began to speak. "Owen, remember that I am only a messenger. My Master wants you to know that He is pleased with your service to Him and that He is pleased that you received your disappointment and trial with faith and patience."

El Bashan paused before continuing. "Your faith has proven that you are strong and you love your God."

Moments later, Helen called Owen to supper. They held hands as Owen said grace. He closed his eyes and bowed his head before saying, "Thank you, Father, for this food. Thank You for keeping evil from our door and giving us confidence in Your proven care of us over all these years. Amen."

After eating his favuorite meal of roast chicken, mashed potatoes with dark gravy, and cucumber salad, Owen kissed Helen on the forehead and stepped back onto the patio, where he slumped into his favourite patio chair.

After Helen had cleared the table and put the remaining food into the refrigerator, she hung her apron on the oven door handle and wiped her damp hands on a towel.

As she stepped onto the patio, she called, "Owen, dear, I hope you enjoyed that meal. You certainly ate your share."

When Owen did not answer, she was sure that he had fallen asleep. But when she touched his arm, he moaned and mumbled indiscernible words.

"Owen! Owen, are you alright?" she shouted.

____

An ambulance arrived, and, after completing a rapid assessment, the paramedics placed an oxygen mask over Owen's nose and mouth and applied EKG leads on his chest. It was only a matter of moments before they had placed him on a stretcher and the ambulance began racing him to the Emergency Room at Foothills Hospital.

Helen's neighbour willingly drove her to the hospital. When she arrived, she was ushered into a family quiet room. After about ten minutes, the door opened, and a physician entered the room.

"I am Dr. Adams," he said. "Are you related to the gentleman who arrived in the ER a short time ago?"

"Yes," responded Helen anxiously. "He's my husband. Will he be alright?"

"I'm afraid I have unpleasant news. It appears that he has had a major cardiac event. Blood tests and an EKG are currently being completed. His medical records indicate that he has had stents placed in two of his coronary arteries. He is currently unconscious, so we will ask you to wait in the family room until he is stable. We will inform you about his condition later."

Eventually a nurse arrived. "Mrs. Richards?"

"Yes."

"Your husband has been transferred to the Cardiac Care Unit."

"What room is he in?"

"He is in CCU Room 510A, but you will not be able to see him for about half an hour."

Helen entered the elevator and pressed the button for the fifth floor. When the door opened, she stepped out and cautiously walked down the well-lit hallway, her eyes apprehensively scanning the small number signs over the entrance to each room. A nurse was restocking a crash cart at the far end of the hallway while a maintenance crew member mopped the shiny floor. A physician wearing a white coat stepped into the hallway, walked over to the nursing station, and began to speak in hushed tones. The hallway and all the rooms were extremely silent.

"Can I help you?" someone asked Helen.

"Yes. I'm looking for 510A," responded Helen.

"Right over there," a young nurse said as she escorted her down the hallway.

"Thank you," whispered Helen.

When she stepped into the room, she took a long breath and clutched her handbag. The bed near the window was empty, so she turned to the bed near the door and saw the sign "510A" on the wall above it. Seeing Owen resting with his eyes closed, she reached out to touch his hand. Owen moaned, but he did not speak or move. She was appalled at the number of tubes and wires that were attached to him. There was a mask over his face delivering vital oxygen, two intravenous lines were attached to his arms, and electrodes for the EKG were fixed to his chest. A cardiac monitor bravely chirped its cadence. Helen reached for the chair next to Owen's bed and slowly lowered herself into the seat. Tears flowed from her eyes while she searched for a tissue in her handbag.

A nurse entered the room and smiled. "Mr. Richards is resting comfortably. Are you a friend or a family member?"

"I'm…I'm his wife, Helen." The words did not flow easily from her quivering lips. She dabbed her eyes with the soft tissue. "Will he recover from this?" she whispered.

"The physician should be here within the next half hour."

The washroom door opened, and a man stepped out of it. He was pushing an IV pole as he shuffled his way to the empty bed next to the window. There, he adjusted his housecoat and lowered himself onto a chair next to the bed.

A few moments later, Helen looked up to see a man standing next to Owen's bed.

"Are you the physician?" she asked.

"No, I am El Bashan. Owen told you about me. He and I have had many conversations, and even though he told you about me, you found it hard to believe that I existed."

Helen could not take her eyes off the white-haired man standing by Owen's bed. "Will Owen die?" she whispered as she stood to her feet.

"I have no authority to make empty promises. The Almighty will guard and keep him, so do not be afraid."

"But…"

"He has just returned from the veil between earthly life and eternal life."

"But…"

El Bashan placed his hand on Owen's leg as Helen dabbed her tearful eyes.

"Will Owen…?"

"Once a person has passed through and into the arena of the redeemed, his reluctance to return to the challenges of earthly life is beyond human comprehension. The Almighty will decide what is best for Owen."

Helen squeezed and patted Owen's hand. The chirping beep emitted by the cardiac monitor maintained its even cadence even as Owen's respiration rate varied in depth and consistency. Helen searched for another tissue to dry her eyes, and when she turned to speak with El Bashan again, he was not there.

Moments later, a woman and a man entered the room.

"I'm Dr. Ganz, and this is Dr. Helman, an intern," the woman said as she reached for the EKG strip. "Mr. Richards has had a major cardiac event. Lab results, along with his cardiac history, indicate that he has had an MI or myocardial infarction. His EKG indicates the seriousness and significance of the MI."

"Now what? Does he need bypass surgery or a heart transplant?"

"Before making that diagnosis, we need to carry out more tests, such as another angiogram."

Dr. Ganz used her stethoscope to listen to Owen's lung sounds and then lifted the sheets from his ankles to check for swelling and edema in his lower extremities.

As the physicians spoke to each other, Helen closed her eyes and began to pray.

Owen stirred, and the EKG emitted a series of unusual sounds. Dr. Ganz reached for the chart on the end of the bed and spent several minutes detailing her findings before both physicians excused themselves and exited the room.

El Bashan reappeared with his hand on Owen's shoulder.

"Are you able to tell me what will happen?" whispered Helen.

"I make no decisions on my own. I am just a servant. I know why you ask, but I have not been informed what to say."

"I know that he will receive eternal life, but..."

"Knowing the immediate future is not always a blessing, but knowing what will ultimately occur is invaluable. I have been assigned to remain with Owen, so take comfort. My Master never intends to bring despair to His servants, but He desires that you trust His decisions."

Helen placed her palm on Owen's forehead. "Owen, if you can hear me, God loves you, and so do I."

Helen leaned over and kissed Owen's forehead before closing her eyes and slumping back into the chair next to Owen's bed. Her vigil had begun. Yes, she had faith that all would be well, but fear still gripped her. What would life without Owen be like? She could not bear to think about it, so she tightened her grip on Owen's hand as if to force him to get up and be well and strong again.

Once again, the lonely night drew her into an uncomfortable embrace.

————————

Chapter 15
O Owen, My Husband

Darkness surrounded the hospital, and the hallway remained silent and empty, except for when one of the nursing staff would glide along it on some unknown mission. From time to time, one would enter the room and check Owen's vital signs.

Toward morning, after one of these visits, a nurse offered Helen a cup of tea and asked her to accompany her to the family room.

"Several staff need to attend to your husband," the nurse said, "so please remain here until they summon you." She closed the door as Helen sipped her hot drink.

After some time, Helen became anxious. She was about to go to the nurses' station when the door opened.

"Mrs. Richards, we have not forgotten you," a nurse said. "Please be patient with us. We will summon you at the appropriate time."

Another hour passed, and Helen decided to go to Owen's room. Stepping into the room, she was shocked to see that Owen's bed was empty. The bed had fresh linen on it, and it was neatly made up. She blinked her eyes as she searched for the sign above the bed.

"They must have moved him," she whispered to herself.

When she stopped at the nursing station, a nurse looked at her. "Are you Mrs. Richards?"

"Can you tell me where they have taken Owen?"

"Mrs. Richards, please follow me."

Helen was not expecting to arrive in the family room again.

"Mrs. Richards, your husband has passed away. I'm sorry."

"Oh, no," Helen whispered. "Oh, Owen! I was not there for you."

"A relative of yours was with him," interjected the nurse.

"But we have no relatives...Owen has no relatives in Calgary."

"A white-haired gentleman was standing next to the bed as the team tried to provide assistance. Dr. Ganz made every attempt to resuscitate your husband, but..."

"Where is Owen now, and where is that white-haired man?" asked Helen.

"The white-haired gentleman was walking with the porters as they escorted your husband down the hallway."

"El Bashan, oh, El Bashan, please take care of my Owen." Helen's words faded into an indiscernible whisper.

Chapter 16
The Granite Epitaph

In a secluded corner of a cemetery in northwest Calgary, Bishop Owen R. Richards rests beneath a modest grey headstone with wind chimes etched into it. Beneath his name, date of birth, and date of death is the phrase:

"A life devoted to obedience
has its own reward."
- Thanks be to God. -

———————

~ *It is now the Beginning.* ~